THE PIRATE KING

KoroN
JAWS
OF DEATH

With special thanks to Allan Frewin Jones

This one is for Toby Saunders

www.beastquest.co.uk

ORCHARD BOOKS
338 Euston Road, London NW1 3BH
Orchard Books Australia
Level 17/207 Kent St, Sydney, NSW 2000

A Paperback Original
First published in Great Britain in 2011

Beast Quest is a registered trademark of Beast Quest Limited
Series created by Beast Quest Limited, London

Text © Beast Quest Limited 2011
Inside illustrations by Pulsar Estudio (Beehive Illustration)
Cover illustrations by Steve Sims © Beast Quest Limited 2011

A CIP catalogue record for this book is available from
the British Library.

ISBN 978 1 40831 311 4

3 5 7 9 10 8 6 4

Printed in Great Britain by CPI Group (UK) Ltd, Croydon, CR0 4YY

The paper and board used in this paperback are natural recyclable
products made from wood grown in sustainable forests. The
manufacturing processes conform to the environmental regulations of
the country of origin.

Orchard Books is a division of Hachette Children's Books,
an Hachette UK company

www.hachette.co.uk

KoroN
JAWS
OF DEATH

BY ADAM BLADE

ORCHARD BOOKS

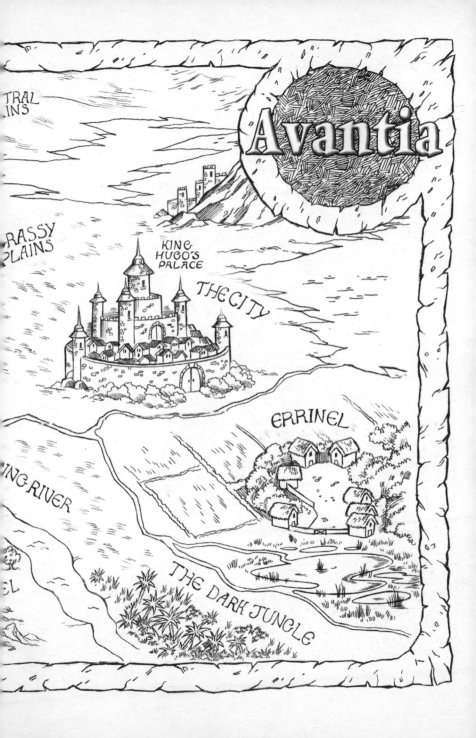

Tremble, warriors of Avantia, for a new enemy stalks your land!

I am Sanpao, the Pirate King of Makai! My ship brings me to your shores to claim an ancient magic more powerful than any you've encountered before. No one can stand in my way, especially not that pathetic boy, Tom, or his friends. Even Aduro cannot help you this time. My pirate band will pillage and burn without mercy, and my Beasts will be more than a match for any hero in Avantia.

Pirates! Batten down the hatches and raise the sails. We come to conquer and destroy!

Sanpao, the Pirate King

PROLOGUE

Abraham stepped slowly towards the skittish mare. "There now, Blizzard," he whispered.

The white horse watched him nervously, her eyes rolling, the breath snorting from her nostrils.

Abraham paused, leaning on his staff. He had been working on the Plains as a horse whisperer since boyhood – but this magnificent mare was his most troublesome adversary yet. He could see she had a powerful spirit.

"So, you threw your last rider," he murmured. "And every rider before him, I'll warrant. And you broke down a fence to escape." He clicked his tongue. "That will never do."

The horse bared her teeth, stamping the ground as if she was on the brink of bolting.

"I'll do you no harm," Abraham said, moving forwards again. He was almost upon her now. He reached out an open hand.

Her head dipped and she sniffed his palm, her eyes softening. Abraham came in close, stroking her muscular neck. He lifted the trailing reins.

"That wasn't so bad, was it?" he whispered, getting on to her back. "I'll have you back in the village in no time."

A shadow loomed over them and

Abraham heard a dreadful snarl. The horse's head jerked up, a sharp light igniting in her eyes. She reared on her hind legs, hooves kicking the air, throwing Abraham off. He got up and grabbed her reins, struggling to control her.

He turned and his blood froze as he stared up at a gigantic Beast leaping towards them. It was like a tiger – black as midnight with slashes of blood-red fur across its body – but it was at least three times the size of any tiger he had ever seen.

The great Beast came crashing down a few paces away. Scythe-like claws raked the ground. The fur bristled at the Beast's neck as it drew back its black lips to reveal teeth like daggers. Thick drool dripped from the points of its teeth – hissing and smoking as it scorched the grass.

But even as Abraham tried to understand what he was seeing, his eyes were drawn upwards in horror. Arching high above the monster's back was a thick scorpion-like tail, scaly and tipped with a vicious sting

that dripped green poison.

Abraham scrambled back, not daring to look away. The creature padded forwards, moving slowly, its muscular body rippling. Abraham heard Blizzard snorting and blowing behind him.

The monstrous cat's eyes bored into Abraham. He could hear its harsh breath rasping in its throat, as though its lungs were great bellows.

The Beast roared, jaws gaping. Its stinking breath blasted into Abraham's face. It pounced, rearing high above them and coming down with its claws spread wide and its dripping fangs bared.

Abraham dived aside with a cry of terror. The edge of one massive paw struck him on the shoulder, knocking him to the ground. He watched helplessly as the Beast's claws raked across Blizzard's back, ripping through the flesh. The horse shrieked in pain as she stumbled away.

Abraham staggered to his feet, beating at the tiger-Beast's flanks with his staff. The monster turned, as quick and lithe as any cat, and before Abraham could move, the staff was gripped between its jaws.

Snap! The staff splintered, and now the monster's eyes turned to Abraham.

But even as the Beast's jaws widened to tear apart his body, he saw Blizzard turn her back to the great cat and lash out with her powerful hind legs. The Beast yowled in anger and pain, twisting to face the horse, its sting rising, and pulsing with poison.

"Run!" shouted Abraham. "Run for your life!"

Blizzard whinnied and pounded across the grasslands. With a shivering snarl, the Beast went leaping after her, its high tail lashing.

Abraham gasped for breath as he watched the two creatures race away. He doubted that even such a horse as Blizzard could outrun the fearsome Beast.

Then, a curious whirling, churning sound made him stare upwards. His mouth gaped in astonishment.

"It cannot be!" he gasped.

Sweeping down from the high heavens, its sails billowing and its flag cracking in the wind, was a flying ship!

CHAPTER ONE

THE ENCHANTED WIZARD

Two days had passed since Tom and Elenna had encountered the Pirate King Sanpao and defeated the sea Beast he had set upon them. It had been a fierce battle with a wily and treacherous foe, and Tom worried that worse was to come.

They were riding through the northern reaches of the Forest of

Fear, making for the Grassy Plains and the next stage of their Quest. The air was stifling under the thick branches, and eerie noises came drifting out of the gloomy shadows.

"I wish Silver were with us," said Elenna.

Tom nodded solemnly, knowing how hard it must be for her to be without her noble wolf companion. "We've both lost someone," he said, thinking of his mother, who was also trapped in Tavania. "The only way to free them is to find the Tree of Being."

"That won't be easy," Elenna said angrily. "Not without Aduro."

She was right. The Good Wizard who'd been their friend and guide over so many past Quests was now in thrall to the Pirate King. And Tom's valiant father, Taladon, could not come to their aid either: he lay injured in King Hugo's castle.

Tom's hand moved to his waist, reminding him of something else he had lost. Aduro had stolen his jewelled belt from him and given it to Sanpao, and now the Pirate King controlled the powers of the coloured jewels.

Aduro had used his magic to place a sash of raw animal hide around Tom's waist. Tom had tried to take it off, but it was impossible. Tucked into the sash was a claw that had floated up to him from the Water Beast, Balisk.

"We're on our own," Tom muttered darkly. "Or *almost* on our own. At least we have one thing to guide us."

"The map," Elenna agreed. "Does it

still show the Tree of Being on the Grassy Plains?"

Tom took the scroll of bark from Storm's saddlebag and unrolled it carefully, revealing the finely etched map of Avantia on its surface. A tiny engraved symbol showed that the Tree was still there – but for how long?

The mystical Tree had the power to open portals into other worlds. But it could also move for its own protection, vanishing in an instant into the ground and sprouting up again elsewhere in the Kingdom. It had looked thin and sickly when they had first seen it, but with Balisk defeated, Tom had noticed that the tree seemed a little stronger.

Their Quest was made more urgent and dangerous by the fact that

Sanpao was also seeking the Tree for his own evil purposes. The Pirate King had already damaged it – tearing away one of its branches to use as a mast for his great galleon. If he had control over the entire Tree, Tom knew that his wickedness would have no limits. He would be powerful enough to take over any kingdom he wished – maybe all of them.

"Tom! Look!" Elenna's voice broke into his thoughts. He followed her pointing finger. A pool of eerie blue light was forming among the trees ahead of them.

Tom reined Storm to a halt, sensing dark magic.

His eyes narrowed as the blur of light writhed and twisted and became a vision of their old friend Aduro, staring out at them from his chamber in King Hugo's castle. Tom shivered to see the cruel smile curling Aduro's lip.

"How is your Quest going, my friends?" he asked mockingly.

Tom felt Elenna's hand on his arm, quietly reminding him that Aduro was under an evil spell. Tom knew that the Good Wizard had a true heart, but it was still hard to see him like this.

"It's going very well, thank you," Tom said in a firm voice. "We will never let Sanpao take the Tree of Being. And we will not rest until my mother and Silver are brought safely home!" He raised his chin defiantly. "Tell that to your pirate master!"

Aduro gave a grating laugh. "Foolish boy," he cackled. "Do you not know that King Sanpao is more

mighty than any foe you have faced
before? You'll never see your mother
or that mangy wolf again!"

Tom's anger took over. "I'll never

give up!" he shouted, plucking Balisk's claw from his sash and hurling it at the vision. The image dissolved and the claw scythed through the blur of blue light, cutting leaves from the forest trees as it went.

Then, to Tom's astonishment, the

claw curved through the air and
came spinning back at him.

He heard Elenna's voice crying out
in fear. "Tom! Be careful!"

The claw hissed as it sliced towards
his face.

CHAPTER TWO

THE WOUNDED HORSE

Tom ducked and the claw thudded into the trunk of a tree behind them. Elenna let out a gasp of relief.

Tom trotted Storm towards the tree, and tugged the claw free. "This could be a useful weapon," he said.

"I wish my arrows came back to me," Elenna exclaimed.

"All the same, I'm glad Aduro was just a vision," Tom said as he tucked it into his leather sash. "I should never have attacked him like that. We have to remember he is under Sanpao's control!"

Riding on through the day, they came at last to the edge of the forest and found themselves in bright daylight. A fresh breeze wafted over the rolling grasslands that spread before them.

But Storm seemed nervous, as though sensing something was wrong. Tom slipped from the saddle and walked over to a patch of grass.

"What is it?" Elenna asked.

Tom crouched, examining the dark red splashes that stained the ground at his feet. "It's blood," he said. He stood up, pointing out across the

Plain. "A trail of blood."

"What could it be?" Elenna asked anxiously. "A wounded person?"

"Whatever it is, I think we should follow it," Tom said.

Elenna jumped down from the saddle and together they walked through the long grass, Storm following as they tracked the spots of blood.

"Can you hear that?" Tom asked after a while. The sound had been getting gradually louder as they walked. *Running water.*

They found themselves in a wide valley, gazing down at a slender silver stream that went dancing over a bed of brown stones.

"I think we've found the wounded animal," Tom said softly.

A white mare stood fetlock deep in

the flowing water, her head lowered to drink. She was saddled and her reins dangled in the water, but there was no sign of a rider. Four parallel wounds ran in a ragged line down the creature's side, and even as she drank, her blood dripped into the water.

Tom scanned the horizon for

any sign of danger.

"Stay back," said Elenna. "We mustn't frighten her. Let me go first."

Elenna made her way down towards the horse.

The mare's head rose suddenly and she turned, ears laid back, tail flicking nervously. Tom held his breath. Would the animal bolt? But even at this distance, he could see the light of intelligence in the horse's eyes.

"Oh, you poor thing," Tom heard Elenna say. "Trust me – we'll make you better."

The mare shivered, tossing her mane and shaking her head. But she didn't bolt, and a few moments later, Elenna had the reins in her hands as she stroked the horse's muzzle.

"It's all right," she called to Tom. "You can come now."

As he approached the beautiful animal, Tom could see how badly she had been hurt. Dried blood encrusted the four deep gashes.

"Only a Beast could do that," he muttered. *But what kind of Beast?* he wondered.

Taking the talon of Epos the Flame Bird from the face of his shield, he very gently touched it to the first of the wounds. The mare whinnied and shied away, but Elenna held her steady. Tom ran the talon along the cut, then moved quickly to the next one. Even as he worked on the second wound, he saw the raw lips of torn flesh closing up, mending so completely that in a few moments there was not even a scar or a mark on the horse's white hide.

Tom healed the final wounds, and

the mare's eyes filled with gratitude and relief.

"There," Tom said. "All better." But then something caught his attention. There was another injury, high on the horse's back, behind the saddle. It was different from the long gouges – a painful-looking brand burned into the white hide.

"Sanpao!" Tom hissed angrily, instantly recognising the evil shape of the brand. It was a Beast skull with horns – the mark of the Pirate King.

"The Pirates did this?" Elenna gasped. "Are they here already?"

"They must be," exclaimed Tom. He snatched out the map, his finger following the route they had taken from the forest to the stream. If the map was accurate, then the Tree of

Being was close by – only a short
gallop away.

"We may still be in time!" he said,
running to Storm and leaping into
the saddle. "Elenna – stay with the
horse. I have to find the Tree!"

He urged Storm into a canter up
the long grassy slope. There was no
time to lose! He couldn't let the
pirates reach the Tree of Being first.

As he approached the crest of the
hill, he heard the thud of hooves
behind. He turned his head, surprised
to see Elenna riding the white horse,
and catching up fast.

Side by side, they came to the
hilltop. The undulating plain
stretched away to the far horizon.

"We should be able to see the Tree
now!" Tom shouted, staring
desperately out over the grasslands.

He pointed to a hollow at the foot of the hill. "It should be right there!"

"I don't understand," said Elenna.

Tom turned grimly to her. "I think I know what this means," he growled. "Sanpao has already been here – he's taken the Tree!" Anger and frustration boiled up in him. "It means we've failed."

CHAPTER THREE
DIRTY TRICKS

"Who's that?" Elenna was pointing along the ridge of the hill. A man stood there, dressed in peasant clothes and waving at them.

"He may have seen what happened," said Tom as they rode along the ridge.

"You found her, thank goodness!" said the man, nodding to the horse as they came to a halt in front of him.

"Her name is Blizzard, and mine is Abraham. I've been searching for her." He frowned, obviously puzzled. "But she was wounded: the claw-marks...?"

"There's no time to explain," Tom said, spotting a curious, unsettling light in the man's eyes. He had seen it somewhere before – but where? "Have you seen anything unusual on the Plains?" he asked.

"I have seen horrors and nightmares in my homeland," Abraham replied with a grimace. "I was attacked by a Beast." His eyes widened. "But then I saw something impossible. A flying ship! A great galleon with a crew of men bearing strange curved swords."

"We've met them before," growled Tom. "They're pirates, and their leader is a man named Sanpao. Did you see where they went?"

"Their ship made for my homestead," said Abraham. "I fear they'll plunder my house and steal my horses."

"Is it far?" asked Tom.

"At the gallop, we could be there very quickly," said Abraham.

"Elenna," said Tom. "Climb up behind me on Storm – let Abraham ride Blizzard." He turned to the man. "Take us to your home."

They'd only been galloping over the plain for a short while when Tom saw an isolated farmstead in front of them. There was a house and a barn, and several paddocks with high fences and strong wooden gates.

But the paddock gates were open and there was no sign of any horses.

Reining Blizzard up, Abraham slipped down from the saddle, falling to his knees, with his fists raised in despair. "They have already been here!" he cried. "All my horses have been taken!"

Tom and Elenna dismounted. Elenna looked into Tom's eyes and he knew exactly what she was thinking. *Too late, again!*

Abraham staggered to his feet and stumbled into one of the enclosures. "All is lost!" he cried. "I'm ruined!"

Tom and Elenna followed him into the corral.

"You're alive, and that's something," Elenna told him. "The Beast or the pirates might have killed you!"

The man turned, his eyes burning. "They might," he exclaimed. "But they didn't!" And with that, he ran past them, sending them both spinning. Tom knew that something was wrong – but before he could even draw his sword, Abraham had dashed through the gate and had swung it closed behind them. The iron bolt clanged as he threw it across.

"You tricked us!" Tom raged, hurling himself at the gate. He could see Abraham's gleaming eyes through gaps in the planking. Now he knew where he had seen that strange light before. In the eyes of Aduro!

"Let us out," shouted Elenna.

"It's useless talking to him," Tom spat. "He's under Sanpao's spell!"

Outside the corral, Storm neighed loudly.

"You won't keep us locked up here for long!" Tom shouted to Abraham. He began to climb the gate, with

Elenna only a fraction behind him.

"I don't need to," Abraham cried. "Can't you hear? They're coming!"

Tom reached the top of the gate as a dreadful sight met his eyes. A great band of pirates – a score or more – galloped in from all sides, their ponytails floating out behind them. As they raised their curved swords high, they howled ferocious war-cries.

The two friends climbed over the gate and jumped down on the other side. Abraham was watching the pirates with a triumphant grin on his face. The horses the pirates were riding must have come from the empty corral, Tom realised.

"Stay close to me," he warned Elenna as he drew his sword and lifted his shield. "We have to make

a run for Storm. We may still be able to ride between them."

Elenna had an arrow to her bow as the two of them sped towards the waiting horse.

The pirates drew up sharply, their eyes flashing and their swords bright and cruel in the sunlight. They had the farmstead surrounded. To get past them, Tom and Elenna would have to battle for their lives.

But even as they neared Storm, a deep shadow loomed over them and a voice boomed out from above: "Stop!"

Tom looked up as the Pirate King's galleon came racing across the sky, like a great flying castle, fortified with turrets and battlements. Its blood red sails billowed, the Beast skull flag snapping in the wind. As Tom gazed up at the dreadful sight, he saw the Pirate King himself staring down at them.

"We meet again!" Sanpao called. "Trust me – this time will be the last!"

CHAPTER FOUR

BETRAYED BY A FRIEND

The terrible pirate ship came thundering down, crushing the wooden walls of the paddocks with its slimy, barnacled hull. The vessel's sails rippled and its timbers groaned as it came to a halt, looming over the farmstead like a hideous mountain of wood, canvas and iron.

Tom and Elenna sprang back as a

gangplank was pushed down. Storm
and Blizzard whinnied in alarm, and
Abraham was on his knees with his
arms spread in greeting. The Pirate
King appeared at the ship's rail.

"My master!" Abraham whined.
Tom's fist tightened around his sword
hilt, and at his side he saw that
Elenna was ready with her bow.

But they were surrounded. How

could they hope to win a fight against so many? "Don't shoot him," Tom murmured to Elenna. "Let's wait for a better chance to escape."

Tom eyed the Pirate King with contempt as he came stamping down the gangplank. The skin on Sanpao's face and neck and arms was stained with dark tattoos and his long ponytail hung down his back, studded with sharp iron darts.

A vicious grin stretched across Sanpao's scarred face. His cutlass was sheathed, and he carried a huge double-headed axe across his powerful shoulders.

He's still wearing my belt! Tom thought angrily, seeing the jewels glinting at the Pirate King's waist.

Sanpao towered over Tom and Elenna. All around them, the

mounted pirates roared. "Greetings to our great King! Greetings to Sanpao the unconquerable!"

"How shall I reward your insolence, boy?" he growled. "Should I slice your head clean off your shoulders? Or something more amusing? Cut your body into small pieces for the entertainment of my crew?"

Tom stared steadily into his face. As before, he noticed how the pirate's left eye was half closed, the lid pressed down by thick scar tissue.

"Do your worst!" said Tom. "I'm not afraid of you."

Tom scanned the vessel quickly and his spirits lifted a little. There was no sign of the Tree of Being on the ship. Blizzard snorted and skittered backwards.

"There she is," said Sanpao. "We branded the nag, but she escaped again."

"Maybe she can smell evil," hissed Elenna.

"Listen to her!" howled one of the pirates. "Kill them, sire! Cut them into chops! Boil their bones and feed 'em to the dogs!"

"You should have stayed away from me, boy," spat Sanpao. "You and your feisty friend. Ha! See how she glares at me! Would you like to fire an arrow at me, missy? You'd be dead before it struck!"

"It might be worth it to rid the world of you!" snarled Elenna, raising her bow and aiming an arrow straight at the Pirate King's heart.

"Brave words, girl!" laughed Sanpao.

"Lower your bow, Elenna," Tom

whispered. "This isn't the way."

"Wisely said," said Sanpao. "But empty your mind of any thoughts of escape. You will die, and how you behave will dictate whether your deaths are swift or prolonged. But in the meantime, I have other duties to attend to." He bared his teeth in a fierce grin. "My pet wizard has told me that the Tree of Being will appear near here very soon." He raised a clenched fist. "I will take its power for my own, and there is nothing you two can do to stop me!"

Anger and hatred welled up in Tom. Yelling with rage, he flung himself at the Pirate King, hoping desperately to deliver a killing blow before he was cut down.

Sanpao stepped neatly aside. The great battleaxe was off his shoulder

in an instant, sweeping through the
air and striking against Tom's shield.
Tom swung his sword. It rang against
the axe, but he was allowed only one
blow before the Sanpao thrust his
axe-head forward into Tom's chest,
knocking him over.

Undaunted, Tom leaped to his feet,
ready to attack again.

"Tom! Watch out!" Elenna cried,
and at the same moment Tom saw
Storm springing forward from where

he had been standing at Blizzard's side. For a moment, he thought the noble horse was coming to his aid, but suddenly the stallion turned and let fly with his back legs.

Stunned, Tom only just had time to bring his shield up to block the kick. Storm's hooves struck against his shield, hurling him backwards so that he fell and rolled helplessly almost to the Pirate King's feet.

"Storm! No!" shouted Elenna.

But her voice was drowned by the hideous cheering of the pirates and by Sanpao's bellowing laughter.

Tom's mind was still reeling. What had happened? Had the loyal animal struck out blindly, thinking he was aiming for the Pirate King?

Sanpao called out. "To me, my faithful steed! Come to your master!"

Storm trotted obediently to Sanpao, and now Tom could see the eerie light that gleamed in the animal's eyes. *Just like Abraham and Aduro!*

The Pirate King swung himself up into the saddle, dragging back on the reins and digging his heels cruelly into Storm's flanks. The horse reared and neighed, foam flying from his lips.

Sanpao glared down at him. "You see, boy? There is nothing of yours that I cannot take. Nothing!"

As Tom lay in the dirt and saw the pirate's evil spell flickering in Storm's eyes, he began to fear that Sanpao may be right. But the doubts only troubled him for an instant. The next moment he was up on his feet, sword ready, his shield steady on his arm. Even if this Quest were to be the death of him – he would not give up.

CHAPTER FIVE

THE SHIP
OF DEATH

As Tom rushed at the Pirate King,
Sanpao forced Storm to rear up and
lash out with his hooves. Tom moved
in, dodging to avoid the thrashing
hooves and the long swings of
Sanpao's axe. If he could just manage
one good thrust with his sword!

But the amber jewel of the
mammoth, Tusk, was glowing at

Sanpao's waist, boosting his battle skills, and Tom was unable to get past his guard.

He's using my own powers against me! thought Tom. *I'll make him pay for that.*

Storm's flailing hoof crashed against Tom's shield, driving him to his knees. As he fought to get to his feet again, the axe struck Tom's sword from his hand, sending it spinning through the air. Sanpao jumped down from the saddle and ripped Tom's shield from his arm, bringing the blade of his axe to a halt a hair's breadth from Tom's neck.

Panting, Tom stared up at Sanpao.

"Enough of this!" shouted the Pirate King. He stared up at his ship. "Kimal! My first mate – I leave you in charge. Do what you will with these weak *children*! I must go and

await the coming of the Tree!"

Sanpao tossed Tom's shield away and
sprung onto Storm's back. He
wrenched on the reins and then
turned and galloped off, heading
towards the hollow under the hill,
where the Tree of Being was to appear.

Elenna had already been grabbed
by pirates and her bow and quiver of
arrows had been torn from her. The

pirates hauled Tom to his feet. He felt
disheartened and ashamed to have
failed so completely. The Pirate King
had his belt *and* his horse.

*And it won't be long before he has the
Tree of Being*, thought Tom.

Tom struggled as the pirates tied
ropes around him, but there were too
many of them and soon his arms
were pinned helplessly to his sides.

"You cowards!" shouted Elenna.
"Give us our weapons and fight us
one-to-one!" But the pirates just
laughed at her as they knotted more
ropes around their ankles. Tom
couldn't do a thing as the pirates
lifted them shoulder-high and carried
them up the gangplank to the ship.

Tom strained against the ropes as
the pirates threw the two friends
down onto the deck. He winced in

pain as he struck the boards, and he heard Elenna groan. Fortunately, they were close together and facing one another. Tom looked into Elenna's eyes, seeing fear in them. A trickle of blood ran from her lip.

"We'll think of something, don't worry," Tom whispered. His words were cut off by a kick in the back.

"Be quiet, you rats!"

Tom stared up at the first mate. Kimal was a huge brute, his bare chest crisscrossed with scars, his skull patterned with evil-looking tattoos.

"Release me and give me my sword, and you'll soon see how this rat fights back!" Tom snarled.

Kimal threw back his head and laughed. "You'll beg for a swift death by the time we are done with you," he said. "But first things first." He turned, shouting to his crew. "Bring the horses aboard."

The timbers of the pirate ship boomed as the mounted pirates came pounding aboard. As the gangplank was drawn up, Tom noticed that Blizzard was not among the horses. The fierce mare must have proved too hard to handle.

Good for her! Tom thought.

Kimal took Tom and Elenna by the scruff of their necks and dragged them to their feet. He brought them to the ship's rail as the red sails filled and the ship shuddered in preparation for flight.

"Tie them to the gunwales," Kimal ordered. Two pirates came forwards and bound Tom and Elenna's feet to the ship's rail. Then, with its sails stretching and its ropes humming, the huge galleon rose into the air.

"Where are you taking us?" Elenna demanded.

"Would you like a better view?" Kimal asked. "I think that can be arranged." He grasped each of them in one of his massive fists and lifted them off the ground.

Shaking with laughter, he heaved them over the rail.

Tom's legs thrashed in the air as he stared down. The ground shrank away, far below. For a moment he hung there at Elenna's side, his feet dangling, and then, to his horror, Kimal let go. They plunged downwards. Tom's ears were filled with the hissing of the wind, and his stomach turned over and over.

Half-way to the ground, the ropes pulled them up sharply, biting into Tom's ankles, jarring his body, and making him cry out in agony. Elenna hung at his side, upside down. Laughter drifted down from the ship. Tom twisted his head and saw the faces of the pirates staring down at them as they swung helplessly in the wind. He saw one of them hurl something. It was a knife. It sliced the air close to the taut rope.

So that was the plan! The pirates were playing a vicious game with them – and the sport would only end when the two of them were sent tumbling helplessly to their deaths.

"Again!" shouted Kimal. "A golden coin to the man who cuts them loose!"

CHAPTER SIX

SKULLS AND HOOVES

Tom felt dizzy and disorientated as he twisted at the end of the long rope. More knives spun past and the pirates yelled and cheered. It would only be a matter of time before one of the knives struck home and the ropes were cut.

And then I will never find the Tree of Being, he thought desperately.

My mother and Silver will be trapped for all time!

The pirate ship cleaved through the sky, passing over dense forests and rocky outcrops. Tom ground his teeth in frustration, the blood thundering in his head, the ropes cutting into his flesh. All the time, the Tree of Being was getting further away. But then he saw that their flight was taking them towards a great lake that stretched out to the north of the Plains.

An idea formed in his mind. He strained against the ropes that bound his arms to his sides. They loosened a fraction and he was able to worm his hand up to his chest. His fingers closed around the claw in his sash and he cautiously edged it out.

"Don't drop it," warned Elenna, watching him intently and

understanding what he was trying to do.

He began to saw at his bonds.

One by one the strands of rope came free. They were almost over the water now and he was unbound save for the ropes around his ankles. So far the pirates hadn't noticed what Tom was doing. He could hear them shouting at one another; they were busy making wagers on who would win Kimal's gold coin. A thrown knife slashed dangerously close to his face and another tore a slice from Elenna's sleeve.

"Ha!" roared a pirate. "The gold coin is almost mine!"

Tom finally split the ropes on his wrists and shook his hands free. Kimal's voice rose above the others. "The boy is cutting through the ropes! Kill them! Kill them both, now!"

Tom had to act quickly. He swung himself towards Elenna and caught hold of her, sawing at the ropes around her chest. He could hear the pirates shouting and howling. More knives came hurtling down. The pirates were no longer aiming at the ropes – their targets were Tom and Elenna's dangling bodies.

Tom saw the waters of the lake glistening below them now.

"Trust me!" he gasped as he cut the rope around Elenna's feet.

"Always!"

She fell, lifting her arms over her head as she scythed down into the water. A moment later Tom sawed through his own rope and plunged after her.

The water was freezing. Bubbles filled Tom's vision as he sank deeper and deeper. He twisted in the darkness, striking upwards, his lungs aching for air, his head pounding.

He broke the surface with a gasp, still clutching the claw in his fist, treading water as he turned his head this way and that in search of Elenna. Where was she? Had she drowned?

"Elenna!" he called frantically.

There was a rush of water close by him and his friend's head appeared.

"I'm all right!" she panted, her hair sticking to her face, and a defiant gleam in her eyes.

Tom pushed the claw back into his sash and, keeping close together, they swam for the shore. Tom looked up as they clambered out of the lake.

The pirate ship had turned and the crew were busy on deck with some large object that they were hauling to the rail.

"What is that?" Elenna asked. "It's not the bone crossbow they used before."

"I think it's a catapult," Tom said. "They're loading it! We have to run!"

He saw the pirates place a white object on the firing arm of the weapon. A moment later the catapult released with a sharp snapping sound. The white object came spinning towards them.

It was a human skull! Tom pushed Elenna to one side then dived in the opposite direction as the horrible missile crashed into the ground and exploded into fragments of bone.

Tom scrambled to his feet, pulling

Elenna up in her dripping clothes.

Another skull shot down at them, landing with a splash in the shallow water.

"Run!" Tom shouted.

They raced over the uneven

ground, zigzagging to avoid being easy targets. All the while, the ship loomed nearer, casting its massive shadow across the ground.

"Run them down!" bellowed Kimal.

Tom heard a whistle beside his head as one of the skulls thumped into the ground beside him. "They're getting closer!" he called to Elenna.

They leaped over a ditch, and Tom grabbed Elenna's arm, veering aside along the length of the channel.

"Bring us about!" shouted Sanpao's first mate. The ship creaked and the sails snapped with the sudden manoeuvre. Tom had bought them some time. He and Elenna charged and stumbled over the uneven ground, until suddenly he heard hooves. The ground began to shake under his feet, as though a thousand cattle were stampeding towards them.

"It's Tagus!" shouted Elenna as the huge Beast came galloping into view. His man's chest heaved and his horse's flanks glistened with sweat as he came pounding towards them, lifting one powerful arm in greeting.

Glad as he was to see the Good Beast, Tom had a sense of foreboding

as he remembered that Sanpao commanded evil Beasts of his own. How long would it be before the Pirate King unleashed one of his fearsome Beasts on them?

"Tagus came without being summoned!" Tom cried. Never in his life had he been so pleased to meet an old friend. The ship was coming straight for them, and Kimal gripped the deck-rail, his face set in a scowl.

"He must have seen the ship," Elenna said. "Thank you, Tagus!"

Tagus came to a halt, growling in greeting as they clambered up on to his back. But the ship was so close now that Tom could smell the rotting filth that caked its hull.

The pirates sent another skull missile hurtling down. It burst into bony shards close by Tagus's front hoof.

"Go!" Tom shouted, digging his heels into the Beast's broad flanks. He leaned forwards, pointing back the way they'd come. "That way, Tagus!"

Although the Beast didn't understand human speech, he understood what Tom wanted. Tom and Elenna clung on desperately as Tagus took off at a gallop.

Tom looked up. The pirate ship was close behind, its sails straining as it raced after them.

"Run while you can!" Kimal cried. "You won't escape us! We'll pursue you to the ends of the world!"

Even as the dreadful threat echoed in Tom's ears, he saw a skull speeding directly towards him. He was unarmed and his shield was gone. He had no hope of avoiding the deadly missile!

CHAPTER SEVEN

THE BEAST COMES

Tagus twisted to one side at the very
last moment. The skull grazed past
Tom's shoulder and broke into jagged
fragments in the grass. But the ship
was gaining at an alarming speed.
It's terrible shadow swept over them
as it cleaved through the air.

Tom leaned forward, shouting at
the top of his voice. "Tagus! You have
to run quicker!"

The Horse-Man gave a snort, his brawny arms pumping the air. Tom hung on grimly to the Good Beast's waist as Tagus put on a sudden spurt of speed. Elenna's hands gripped his waist.

"We should retrieve our weapons," he heard her shout against the wind of their wild gallop.

"Go that way, Tagus!" Tom shouted, pointing. The Beast nodded and veered to one side, and it was all Tom could do to stay on his back as he went careering over the plain towards Abraham's farmstead.

Tom risked a look over his shoulder. The pirate ship was falling behind now, and he could see Kimal roaring in frustration as he swung the wheel to try and keep up with them. They reached the farmstead

and Tom shouted for Tagus to pull
up. The Good Beast halted so
suddenly that Tom was almost hurled
into the grass. The Horse-Man's chest
and flanks rose and fell as he caught
his breath, and there was a fierce

smile on his face as Tom and Elenna jumped down and searched for their weapons.

Tom found his shield and sword, and Elenna her bow and quiver just beside the shattered corral. Tom glanced up at the sky, seeing the pirate ship closing in on them again.

Elenna notched an arrow to the string and pulled it back, her knuckles whitening on the bow. Her arms trembled a little as she held it taut. She closed one eye, aiming along the shaft of the arrow, holding her breath. The bow steadied in her hands, then she shot.

The shaft sped swift and true up towards the ship. It struck Kimal in the shoulder. He staggered back, bellowing in pain, and losing his grip on the wheel. The great hoop of wood spun out of control and the pirate ship sheered away, twisting to one side and tipping forwards so that the crew fell about the decks.

"Great shot!" Tom declared, smiling at Elenna.

"I hope so," Elenna replied, watching anxiously as the doomed ship plunged towards the ground.

Kimal lunged at the wheel, grasping it in both hands to hold it steady. The prow of the great ship lifted and the decks began to level. But not enough.

With an impact that shook the ground, the keel ploughed into the grass with a deafening crash, churning up huge clods of earth. The ship came to a grinding halt.

To Tom's dismay, he saw that it was undamaged. But there was panic

aboard as the newly captured horses
broke free and began to gallop across
the deck and leap over the gunwales
to freedom.

"I don't think they'll be bothering

us for a while," Tom said with grim satisfaction as he saw Kimal trying vainly to muster his men. "Now we can face Sanpao!"

Elenna and Tom sprang up on to Tagus's back again. As though the Beast knew what was needed from him, he broke into a gallop – and this time he was heading straight for the place where the Tree of Being should have appeared.

"It's already there!" cried Tom as they rode up the hill. The Tree was unmistakeable. It soared into the sky, towering over the Plains, taller than any tree Tom had ever seen. Tom could see that it was no longer dying. The branches, though still bare, stood out more proudly from the trunk, and there were fewer patches of disease on the bark.

But as they came to the crest of the hill, he saw that the tree was in deadly peril.

Sanpao stood at its base, the double-headed battleaxe in his hands. And Abraham was with him, wielding a smaller axe.

"They're going to chop the tree down!' cried Elenna.

Worst of all, Storm stood quietly to one side with Blizzard, both horses still trapped in the Pirate King's thrall, their eyes glowing eerily.

"Sanpao!" Tom shouted. "Stop!"

At his back, Elenna levelled an arrow as Tagus cantered down the hill towards the two men.

Sanpao rested his axe on his shoulder, watching them approach. If he was surprised or alarmed at the sight of the Good Beast, he didn't show it. A grin spread across his scarred face.

The Pirate King drew in a deep breath and let out a shout. "Koron!"

"What's Koron?" Elenna asked.

Tom pointed to a creature that was approaching them at great speed across the Plains. "He is, I think!" he said.

The massive, tiger-like Beast had black fur streaked with ugly red markings, and stiff hairs bristled like wire around his neck. The loathsome yellow slits of his eyes burned with malice, and his black lips were drawn back from drooling fangs. Where his thick spittle hit the grass, it left smoking scorch marks. Great claws gouged the ground as he bounded towards the Tree, roaring ferociously. A scaly, curving tail lifted over the fearsome Beast's back, ending in a terrible sting that glistened with green venom.

Tom drew his sword, preparing for the fight of his life. But Koron was not heading for them – he bounded towards the Pirate King. Hope grew in Tom's heart. Despite his monstrous appearance, might Koron be a Good Beast? Might he attack Sanpao?

The Pirate King was still staring up at Tagus and the two friends, almost as if he was unaware of the huge Beast bearing down on him. But then, at the last possible moment, Sanpao turned, flexing his knees and spreading his arms.

Tom watched in amazement as the Pirate King leaped into the air. He back-flipped with supple strength over the Beast's head, and landed easily astride the monster's shoulders.

Sanpao brandished his axe. "Dare
you face me now, boy?" he shouted.
"Dare you face Koron, Jaws of
Death?"

CHAPTER EIGHT

THE BLINDING VENOM

Tom lifted his sword high. "I don't fear you or your Beast!" he shouted to the Pirate King. He turned quickly to Elenna. "Jump down," he said. "Make sure Abraham can't do any harm to the Tree with that axe of his. Tagus and I will deal with Sanpao!"

"Be careful!" Elenna said as she dropped from the Good Beast's back.

"Sanpao is dangerous enough on his *own*."

Tom narrowed his eyes as he turned back to his enemies. "Tagus! Take me to them!" he called. "Let's show them how we fight!"

Koron turned now and came pounding up the hill towards Tom and his friends. The Beast's slavering mouth gaped wide, spitting deadly drool, the yellow fangs bared like great curved daggers. And as he ran, the scaly tail lashed from side to side above his back, spraying vile green venom.

Tagus reared up with a roar, and careered down the hillside towards Koron and the Pirate King. Tom clung onto the Beast's wide back, and lifted his shield.

I have to defeat Sanpao and his Beast, Tom thought grimly. *If the Tree of*

Being is destroyed, I may never see my mother again.

Sanpao let out a shrill cry as Koron loped up the hillside.

"Attack!" shouted Tom, as the four enemies rushed at one another. "For Freya and for Silver!"

Neither Beast veered off as they came together. Tagus reared up on his strong horse legs, his fore-hooves striking the air. Koron's hairy pelt gave off a sickening, overpowering stench that filled Tom's head and made it hard to concentrate. The evil Beast's jaws snapped, spitting the venomous drool. Sanpao's reach was longer than Tom's and as the Pirate King swung his great axe, Tom had to duck aside to avoid being cut in two. The Beasts grazed past one another, Tagus striking out with his fists and Koron's fangs

gnashing, while above them the
vicious tail lunged and stabbed.

Tom saw that Koron was aiming his
sting at Tagus's face. But the mighty
Horse-Man swung his arm and beat
the tail aside with a bellow of anger.
Tagus was a fearsome fighter, but
Tom wondered how long he could
survive against the speed and
viciousness of Sanpao's Beast.

Sanpao swung the axe again. This

time it clanged against Tom's shield, almost sending him reeling from Tagus's back. But he gripped on tightly with his legs and managed to regain his balance. The two Beasts turned and came together a second time, Tagus roaring in anger, and Koron hissing and spraying thick spittle from his mouth.

This battle was like the jousts that Tom had watched in King Hugo's palace – except that this was no honourable sport and Tom knew only too well that Sanpao wouldn't hesitate to kill him.

Tagus drew back, his teeth bared, his fists pumping the air, breathing hard as he watched the evil Beast's tail swaying above Sanpao's head.

Koron's head dropped, his drool burning the grass. His eyes were on the Good Beast, filled with evil fury. Through the black and red fur, Tom could see the muscles of the Beast's huge body tensing as Koron prepared to spring. On the Beast's back, Sanpao was grinning savagely, as though he knew the battle was already won. Tom stared into Sanpao's face, trying to think of a way to get within striking distance of the Pirate King without falling victim to his huge axe.

The talon of Balisk!

Tom suddenly remembered his new weapon. He sheathed his sword and snatched the claw from his sash, flinging it at Sanpao with all his might. Sanpao jerked to one side, but the claw cut a deep wound high on his right arm. Blood sprayed as the Pirate King howled with pain. The axe fell from his grip, and he rocked sideways on his Beast's back.

A look of absolute rage came over his face as he lost balance and fell, thudding heavily into the long grass.

His heart hammering in his chest, Tom raised his hand to snatch the claw as it came spinning back to him. But as he closed his fingers about it, the claw exploded into fine dust. Tom gave a gasp of dismay. *What had happened?*

He heard the Pirate King roar with laughter. "Did you not know?" he jeered. "The tokens from these Beasts can only be used once! You must fight Koron with nothing but your sword and shield. And they will be little protection for you!"

No sooner had the words left Sanpao's mouth than Koron leaped at Tom and the terrible sting lashed down. Tom lifted his shield to block the blow, feeling the barbed sting strike off the wood, almost unseating him with its force.

Tom sliced with his sword, hoping

to sever the sting. But Koron bounded to one side before the sword could bite, his jaws gaping wide and spraying saliva into Tagus's face.

Tagus let out a bellow of agony. Tom saw smoke rising up from between Tagus's fingers. Patches of the Good Beast's hair had been scorched away, leaving raw wounds.

Howling in pain, the blinded Beast stumbled away across the hillside, his legs buckling, his hands clutching at his sightless eyes. Tagus tripped on a jutting rock and fell heavily onto his side. Tom was thrown off and went rolling down the hill.

Coming to a breathless halt, he felt the ground vibrating under him. He stared up and saw Koron pounding through the air towards him, claws bared and sting poised.

CHAPTER NINE

THE POISONED STING

Tom thrust his shield up, drawing in his head and limbs so that the burning spittle couldn't splash his skin. The face of his shield smoked, but the wood was too powerful to be affected by Koron's saliva. Tom had learned on his battle with Balisk that it was made from the Tree of Being.

The power of the Tree is stronger than

Koron's acid! Tom thought. *At least that's something to be grateful for.*

With a speed and agility honed by countless fights, Tom jumped quickly to his feet again, his sword poised and his shield at the ready.

A guttural laugh made him glance to the side. "Come, Horse-Man!" mocked the Pirate King, standing near the fallen Tagus with his fists on his hips. "Look me in the eyes and you shall see the man who will be your master!"

The blinded Beast struggled vainly to get up, his hands over his eyes, his flesh smouldering.

"That will never happen!" Tom shouted, catching a glimpse of the pitiful wounds on the Good Beast's face. "Tagus will never be your slave!"

Tom wanted desperately to go to his old friend's aid – but there was no time. Koron was crouched low, staring at Tom with raging eyes, the fur around his neck bristling and his sting swaying from side to side.

Sanpao laughed again and pointed to Koron. "All Beasts must do my bidding!"

"But not all *people!*" Tom heard Elenna shout from near the Tree, where she was guarding Abraham with an arrow on the bow-string. "You can beat them both, Tom! I know you can!"

Heartened by Elenna's encouragement, Tom squared up to the Beast, thrusting all other thoughts from his mind.

Koron's lips drew back from his knife-like fangs and his jaws opened in a long, vicious growl. The great claws sank into the ground. Tom spread his legs for better balance, his eyes fixed on the Beast.

Koron sprang, all claws and fangs. Quick as lightning, Tom leaped aside, lunging at the Beast's throat with his sword then darting out of reach of the stabbing sting. The venomous point slashed down a hair's-breadth from his shoulder, spraying poison.

Koron twisted and attacked again. The claws raked down Tom's shield, but again he managed to sidestep and stabbed once more at the Beast's throat. But Koron was too quick to be caught like that. Instead the flat of Tom's blade struck hard against the Beast's muzzle.

Koron retreated a few steps, snarling furiously, shaking his head in pain.

"That's to pay you back for the pain you caused Blizzard!" Tom shouted as he hurled himself forwards and leaped onto the Beast's back. He straddled the hairy neck just as he had seen Sanpao do. If he could stay mounted like this on the Beast, he had the chance to thrust his sword in deep and destroy Koron with one blow.

Koron bucked and thrashed as he tried to throw off his unwanted rider. Tom grasped tufts of fur in each hand, using all his strength just to stay on the crazed Beast. Thrown back and forth and side to side, he could feel every bone in his body being shaken loose and his teeth rattling in his skull.

The angry Beast yowled and spat as it fought to cast Tom off. An instinct made Tom turn and lift his shield. Just in time! He had almost forgotten the whipping tail.

The sting jabbed down, hammering onto the shield and spraying venom. Tom swung his blade over his shield, hoping to sever the sting from the tail. But Koron's tail snapped to the side, striking against his sword and sending it spinning from Tom's hand.

Tom's heart faltered as he clung to the Beast's thick fur. He was unarmed now, and the only protection he had was his shield. Again and again the tail came plunging down. Each time, Tom managed to fend it off. But how long could this go on? How long before Koron managed to throw him off or find a way through his defences?

"Kill him!" Tom heard Sanpao's

voice above the snarls of the Beast. "Mighty Koron! Hurl him off! Rend him with your claws! Break his bones with your teeth! Poison his blood with your sting!"

Cold anger filled Tom – and with the anger came an idea. He had no weapons with which to attack the Beast – but Koron's own weapon might be made to work in his favour.

He twisted, staring upwards, waiting for the tail to lash down again.

He needed to time this perfectly.

Holding his breath, he saw the sting descending. At the last possible moment, he flung himself from the Beast's back. As he had hoped, the unstoppable power of the tail sent the venomous point of the sting deep into Koron's neck.

Tom landed in the grass, rolling over, winded and dizzy. He heard the evil Beast shriek and howl.

"No!" Sanpao bellowed.

Tom climbed to his feet. His plan had worked! Koron was writhing, straining his head around as though trying to bite at the sting embedded in his neck. Strange snarling sounds came from the Beast's flexing jaws.

Suddenly Koron shuddered and slumped to the ground. His black hair faded to a dull grey, and the huge flanks twitched as the legs kicked feebly. The Beast let out a final miserable whine and, as Tom watched in astonishment, Koron dissolved into a mist of fine grey ash that drifted away on the breeze.

The Beast was gone!

CHAPTER TEN

TO FIGHT ANOTHER DAY

"You'll pay for destroying my Beast!" shouted Sanpao. He strode across the hill to where his axe had fallen.

"I don't think so!" called Elenna, turning from Abraham and training her arrow on Sanpao. "One more step and I'll fire!"

The Pirate King glowered at her. "Abraham – use your axe. Kill her!"

Tom darted forwards and picked up his sword. "Elenna – be careful!" he called.

Abraham stared dizzily about himself and then dropped his axe.

"Where am I?" he mumbled.

Tom watched as the Pirate King stood seething with rage. He didn't dare to pick up his axe for fear of being shot by Elenna.

A groan from Tagus reminded Tom of how badly the Good Beast had been hurt. He ran to where the Horse-Man lay, breathing shallowly, his arms over his injured face.

Tom took the talon of Epos from his shield.

"This will help," he muttered gently, then carefully prized the Good Beast's arms from his burned face and laid the healing talon over the red-raw wounds.

Tagus let out a rasping sigh and Tom could tell that the power of the talon was already working. But he had spotted something lying in the grass where Koron had turned to dust. A fang from the Beast's mouth! Tom picked it up and tucked it into his sash, wondering what power it might have.

"Tom, the Tree!" gasped Elenna.

As he finished passing the talon over Tagus's wounds, Tom gazed back down the hill Abraham was leaning against the Tree, as though exhausted from his ordeal under Sanpao's spell. The Tree seemed to be even healthier now than when Tom had first seen it. Small green buds sprouted at the tips of the branches.

"The Tree of Being is starting to

come alive again," Tom murmured in relief. *I'll be able to open the portal and rescue Silver and my mother.* He was about to call out to Elenna to look, when the Tree shuddered from its base to its highest branches.

"No! Stay!" shouted Tom, running down the hill. But the Tree was folding in on itself, its branches closing against the trunk as it began to sink down into the ground. The whole hill shook as the Tree of Being slid swiftly into the earth with a crunching, sucking sound. A few moments later, the grass closed over it and it was as if the Tree had never even been there.

A low laugh made Tom turn angrily. Sanpao was looking gloatingly at him. "Too late!" he crowed. "I'll have that Tree for my own, yet!"

Tom glared at him. "Never," he said. "You'll be tied up and taken back to King Hugo's castle. You can share a dungeon with Malvel – the two of you should get along very well."

Sanpao lifted his head, his eyes burning with malice. "You've only faced two of my Beasts so far," he said. "There are four more – and they're far deadlier than Balisk and Koron."

"Maybe so," declared Tom. "But you'll not be free to control them!"

Sanpao laughed. "You think so?" he said, his eyes moving from Tom's face and staring at something behind and above him.

"Tom!" Elenna's voice cracked like a whip. "The pirate ship!"

Tom turned. The huge galleon was

racing across the sky, its red sails
straining as it drifted towards them.

A rope dangled from the bows.
Before Tom could act, Sanpao leaped
into the air, snatching at the rope.

With a cry of anger, Tom jumped, trying to grab at the Pirate King's boots. But he was too late – the ship was already rising again. Sanpao swarmed up the rope, as agile as a monkey. When he reached the rail, his crew helped him aboard. Then the galleon went skimming away, rising higher and higher into the sky until it was no more than a dot.

Elenna came running up to Tom. "There was nothing you could have done," she said.

A friendly roar sounded behind them. They turned and saw that Tagus was up on his hooves once more, the flesh on his face and shoulders completely healed. Tom ran over to the Good Beast. "Thank you!" he said. "We would never have succeeded without you."

Tagus bowed his head to show he understood Tom's gratitude. Then, lifting one huge hand in a gesture of farewell, he turned and galloped away across the Plains.

"What's happened?" asked a confused-looking Abraham, coming up to the two friends. "I was looking for a horse...for Blizzard. And now..."

They quickly explained how he had been under Sanpao's spell. Abraham shook his head in astonishment. "I'm glad you defeated him!" he declared. "He is an evil man!"

"He hasn't been defeated," Tom said grimly, staring up at the distant dot in the sky. "We have to follow him."

Just then, Storm and Blizzard came trotting up the hill to where they were standing – all trace of Sanpao's dark magic had disappeared from Storm's eyes.

"Take Blizzard with you," said Abraham, smiling at Elenna. "She's already taken a shine to you – you may be the one person she will allow upon her back."

"Thank you," said Elenna. She stroked the white mare's flank, then hoisted herself up into the saddle. Blizzard whickered and dipped her head as if to show Elenna that she was welcome to ride.

Saying goodbye to Abraham, Tom and Elenna cantered off side by side across the Plains in pursuit of the dwindling speck that was Sanpao's pirate ship.

"Wherever Sanpao goes, we go!" Tom said. "We'll make sure he doesn't wreak any more damage in this kingdom."

He flicked the reins, urging Storm into a gallop. Elenna was quick to respond and soon the two companions were racing across the

grasslands after the ship.

While there's blood in my veins, I'll fight every Beast that Sanpao throws at me! Tom vowed.

Join Tom on the next stage
of the Beast Quest where he
will meet

HECTON
THE BODY
SNATCHER

Win an exclusive
Beast Quest T-shirt and goody bag!

Tom has battled many fearsome Beasts and we want to know
which one is your favourite! Send us a drawing or painting of
your favourite Beast and tell us in 30 words why you think
it's the best.

Each month we will select **three** winners to receive
a Beast Quest T-shirt and goody bag!

Send your entry on a postcard to
BEAST QUEST COMPETITION
Orchard Books, 338 Euston Road, London NW1 3BH.

Australian readers should email:
childrens.books@hachette.com.au

New Zealand readers should write to:
Beast Quest Competition, PO Box 3255, Shortland St,
Auckland 1140, NZ or email: childrensbooks@hachette.co.nz

**Don't forget to include your name and address.
Only one entry per child.**

Good luck!

Fight the Beasts,
Fear the Magic

www.beastquest.co.uk

Have you checked out the Beast Quest website?
It's the place to go for games, downloads, activities,
sneak previews and lots of fun!

You can read all about your favourite beasts,
download free screensavers and desktop wallpapers
for your computer, and even challenge your friends
to a Beast Tournament.

Sign up to the newsletter at www.beastquest.co.uk
to receive exclusive extra content and the
opportunity to enter special members-only
competitions. We'll send you up-to-date info on all
the Beast Quest books, including the next exciting
series which features four brand-new Beasts!

All books priced at £4.99,
special bumper editions
priced at £5.99.

Orchard Books are available from all good bookshops, or can
be ordered from our website: www.orchardbooks.co.uk,
or telephone 01235 827702, or fax 01235 8227703.

Series 8: THE PIRATE KING
COLLECT THEM ALL!

Sanpao the Pirate King wants to steal the sacred Tree of Being. Can Tom scupper his plans?

978 1 40831 310 7

978 1 40831 311 4

978 1 40831 312 1

978 1 40831 313 8

978 1 40831 314 5

978 1 40831 315 2

Series 9: The Warlock's Staff
Out September 2011

Meet six terrifying new Beasts!

Ursus the Clawed Roar
Minos the Demon Bull
Koraka the Winged Assassin
Silver the Wild Terror
Spikefin the Water King
Torpix the Twisting Serpent

Watch out for the next Special Bumper Edition

OUT OCT 2011!